THE
Frog Prince

Retold from Grimm
by EDITH H. TARCOV

Illustrated by JAMES MARSHALL

Four Winds Press   New York

For Tara and Joshua
E. H. T.

For Langford Outlaw
J. M.

Library of Congress Cataloging in Publication Data
Tarcov, Edith.
   The frog prince.

   SUMMARY: Angry at being forced to keep her promise to a frog,
the princess finally resorts to violent action with unexpected results.
   [1. Fairy Tales. 2. Folklore—Germany]
   I. Grimm, Jakob Ludwig Karl, 1785-1863. Der Froschkönig.
II. Marshall, James. illus. III. Title.
PZ8.T175Fr   398.2′1′0943 [E]   73-22491

PUBLISHED BY FOUR WINDS PRESS
A DIVISION OF SCHOLASTIC MAGAZINES, INC., NEW YORK, NEW YORK
TEXT COPYRIGHT © 1974 BY EDITH H. TARCOV.
ILLUSTRATIONS COPYRIGHT © 1974 BY JAMES MARSHALL.
ALL RIGHTS RESERVED.
PRINTED IN THE UNITED STATES OF AMERICA.
LIBRARY OF CONGRESS CATALOGUE CARD NUMBER: 73-22491
1 2 3 4 5   78   77   76   75   74

Once upon a time there was a beautiful
princess. She had a golden ball, and it was
her favorite plaything. She took it wherever
she went.

One day the princess was playing in the
woods, near a well. She threw her ball high
into the air. And it fell — splash! — into the
well.

The princess watched her golden ball sink
deep into the water of the well, and she
began to cry. She cried harder and harder.

Suddenly someone said, "What is the
matter, princess? Why are you making so
much noise?"

The princess looked around. She looked into the well.

An ugly little frog was looking up at her. The frog asked again, "What is the matter, princess?"

"Oh it's you, you old water splasher," the princess said. "My golden ball has fallen into the well. That is why I am crying."

"Stop crying," said the frog. "Maybe I can help you. What will you give me if I get your ball for you?"

"I will give you whatever you want, dear frog," said the princess. "Would you like my fine silk dress? Or my necklace of pearls? Or would you like my golden crown?"

"No," said the frog. "What would I do
with your fine silk dress? Or your necklace
of pearls? And what would I do with your
golden crown?"

"What do you want, then?" the princess asked.

The frog looked at the beautiful princess.

He said, "I want to be your friend and playmate. I want to sit with you at the supper table. I want to eat with you from your golden plate and drink with you from your golden cup. I want to sleep on your fine silk pillow. If you promise to let me do these things, I will get your ball for you."

"I promise," the princess said.

She thought, "How can this nasty little frog come to the castle and be my playmate? He has to stay here, in his well." And she said again, "I promise."

Now the frog went down, deep into the well. Soon he came up with the golden ball in his mouth. He threw it onto the grass.

"Oh!" said the princess. "My golden ball!"
She picked it up and ran away.

"Wait, wait!" cried the frog. "Take me
with you! I can't go as fast as you!"

But the princess did not wait. She ran
home to the castle. And soon she forgot all
about the poor little frog.

The next day, at suppertime, the princess sat at the table with her father the king and all the people of the court.

Suddenly everyone heard some strange noises outside.

Splish, splash, splish, splash!

It was the sound of little wet feet coming up the stairs to the castle.

Then,

Flip, flap, flip, flap!

There was a slippery little knock at the door. Someone called:

Princess, princess, open up!
Princess, princess, let us sup!

The princess ran to the door and opened it. When she saw the frog, she shut the door quickly.

The princess came running back to the table. The king looked at her.

"What are you afraid of, daughter?" he asked. "Is there a giant at the door who wants to carry you off?"

"Oh no, Father," said the princess. "It is not a giant. It's a nasty little frog."

The princess told her father how the frog had found her ball. And she told him about her promise.

"I promised I would let him be my friend and playmate," she said. "But I never thought he could come out of the well!"

Flip, flap, flip, flap!

There was that slippery little knock again. And someone called:

"Princess, princess, open up!
Princess, princess, let us sup!
Remember who brought you the ball that fell!
Remember your promise by the well!"

"You must keep your promise, daughter," said the king. "Open the door and let the frog in."

And so the princess had to open the door.

The frog hopped in and followed her to the table. He stopped by her chair.

"Pick me up and put me next to your plate," said the frog.

"Go ahead," the king said. "Do as the frog says. You must keep your promise."

The princess had to put the frog on the table. Everyone could see that she really did not want to do it.

The frog ate with the princess from her golden plate. And he drank with her from her golden cup. The frog liked his supper very much.

But the princess could not eat a thing.

At last the frog said, "Now I am ready to go to sleep. Carry me to your bedroom. And put me on your fine silk pillow."

The princess began to cry.

"Stop crying," said the king. "Do as the frog says. You made a promise, and you must keep it!"

And so the princess had to carry the frog
to her bedroom. She took hold of him with
two fingers, and she put him in a corner.

But the frog said, "I am tired. I want to go to sleep on a fine bed, just like you. Put me on your silk pillow, or I will tell your father."

That made the princess very angry.

She picked up the frog, and she threw him against the wall!

But when he fell to the floor, the frog was no longer a frog.

Now he was a tall prince with beautiful, kind eyes. And he was smiling at the princess.

"A wicked witch turned me into a frog," he said. "But now the spell is broken!"

The very next day the prince and the
princess were married.

A golden coach with eight white horses
drove up to the castle. The prince now took
the princess to his own land. And they lived
there happily forever after.

E
398.2
TAR

E
TAR

cop N

Tarcov, Edith
The frog prince.

Copy 2